Catching BIG BUBBA

LUCKY LUKE'S ADVENTURES

Catching Big Bubba © 2022 by Kevin Lovegreen.
All rights reserved. No part of this book may be reproduced in any form whatsoever, by photography or xerography or by any other means, by broadcast or transmission, by translation into any kind of language, nor by recording electronically or otherwise, without permission in writing from the author, except by a reviewer, who may quote brief passages in critical articles or reviews.

Illustrated by Margarita Sikorskaia

Softcover ISBN 978-1-7370808-4-8
Hardcover ISBN 978-1-7370808-5-5

Printed in the United States of America

Cover and interior design by James Monroe Design, LLC.

Lucky Luke, LLC.
4335 Matthew Court
Eagan, Minnesota 55123

www.KevinLovegreen.com

Quantity discounts available!

Chapter 1

The green grass parts like waves on a lake as I belly crawl toward the water's edge. The magic lake has crystal-clear water. It's up to one thousand feet deep. It's also the home of the largest bass in the world.

She has been seen only two times by local fisherman, but she has never been hooked. Not yet! But today, I'm going to catch her.

I pull myself up to my knees and slide my pure-gold fishing rod off my back. My grandfather gave it to me. He was the king of our fishing village.

I unhook the magic lure that has caught two other world-record bass. It hangs from my pure-gold fishing line. This is the only line strong enough to pull in a bass this big.

I'm ready. I scan the calm water and look for any sign of the monster.

Then I see a giant black mass under the water, like the shadow of a boat. It's moving down the shore, closer to me. My heart beats faster, and my eyes focus on the perfect spot to cast. I slowly arc my fishing rod back and then shoot it forward. It sends the magic lure out into the sky.

The lure lands with a splash, and I begin to reel as fast as I can. The lure races through the water as if trying to escape.

The shadow takes off after the lure like a rocket. This is happening!

Suddenly, a mouth the size of a garbage truck opens up and swallows the lure. With no time to think, I brace my feet and set the hook with all my strength.

The monster bass turns and jumps one hundred feet in the air, yet her tail still touches the water! My eyes grow wide in disbelief. I can't believe she's this big. When she lands, a tidal wave surges up.

As she races for the deep part of the lake, my feet start to slide. I'm being pulled toward the water's edge! The drag on my reel screams, and line is being torn out. Smoke billows from my spool. I'm running out of line! I'm not sure I can hold her!

Then I hear something in the distance.

"Luke, wake up!" says a voice. It sounds like Crystal.

"Luke, wake up," Crystal says again. "It's time to go!"

Several seconds pass while the words sink into my dream. Then my eyes pop open.

I focus on Crystal, standing in my room. She's fully dressed and wearing her yellow jacket.

"Is it time to get up?" I ask, still trying to get my bearings.

"The sun is up, so absolutely," she says excitedly. "Get out of bed already. We're going to the cabin!"

"You have no idea what I was just dreaming," I say, shaking my head.

"Whatever," Crystal says. "I'm heading down for breakfast." She races out of my room.

Then my dream fades away, and a giant smile grows across my face. I remember it's the first day of summer break. We always go to our grandparents' cabin for the first two weeks of break. I can't wait to see Grandma and Grandpa and stay at their amazing cabin tucked way back in the woods. And the lake is awesome! It doesn't have any world-record bass like the one in my dream, but it is full of fish.

My name is Luke. Anyone who knows me knows I love hunting, fishing, and just about anything else in the outdoors. And my grandparents' cabin is one of my favorite places in the world.

Crystal is two years older than me, and she loves volleyball, fishing, hunting, and four-wheeling at the cabin. She has long red hair that reminds me of a lion's mane.

She is about six inches taller than me, but I bet I'll catch her before the end of seventh grade, next year. Mom told me that's when I'll sprout up.

My hair is the same color as Crystal's, but it's a lot shorter. Mom is the only one in our family who doesn't have red hair. She has medium-length dark-brown hair.

I jump out of bed and throw on my blue jeans with the big hole in the knee. I think most of my jeans have holes in them. I then pull on my favorite T-shirt. It's blue and has a big bass on it.

I race down the stairs, skipping every other step. Crystal and Mom are in the kitchen, and I can smell maple sausage cooking. The smell puts an even bigger smile on my face.

Then I notice Crystal. She has a sad look on her face, like she just broke her cell phone or something.

"What's wrong?" I ask.

"We aren't going to the cabin!" she says with a mix of disappointment and a little anger.

"What!" I exclaim. I quickly look at Mom.

"I'm sorry, Luke," Mom says. "Last night your dad got a call, and one of his big projects is having some trouble. He needs to stay and work for a few days, and then we can go up."

"No way! This can't be happening," I say, totally defeated.

Mom gives us both a sympathetic smile. "I know this is disappointing, but you can still have some fun around here."

"But there's nothing to do!" I insist.

"Oh, come on—there's a lot to do around here," Mom replies. "Not all your adventures have to happen up north at the cabin or in the mountains somewhere. It's time to get creative. Let's see what you two can come up with in our own neighborhood!"

"It's not the same, Mom," I say. "This will be the worst start to summer ever!"

"Only if you let it be," Mom says. "Quit thinking negatively. Instead, put your heads together, and come up with some ideas."

I look at Crystal. She's slowly chewing her pancakes.

"What are we going to do?" I ask.

"I have no idea," she says.

Suddenly, a thought pops into my head. "Are Justin and Bart home?" I ask Mom.

Justin and Bart are our cousins, and they live only a few miles away.

"I think so," Mom says, raising both shoulders.

"Should we see if they want to hang out?" I suggest to Crystal.

Her eyes light up, and she tilts her head. "Sure, that could be fun," she says. "I didn't think about that."

"Can I text them, Mom?" I ask with new hope.

"That sounds like a great idea," she replies.

I grab my phone, and my fingers start flying. I text, *Hey, guys! Are you free today? Want to hang out with Crystal and me?*

It feels like hours pass as I wait for a reply. But really, it takes less than a minute for my text alert to ping with a message from Bart.

Yeah! he texts back. *You guys should come fishing with us!*

Hope and excitement build inside me as I read the words. Fishing! But where? How? This is Minnesota, so there are lots of lakes and ponds around our neighborhood. But we've never fished them before.

Awesome! I reply. *We'll head over right after breakfast.*

Bart sends me a thumbs-up and a fish emoji.

I look at Crystal with wide eyes and a crazy smile.

"Eat up!" I say. "We're going fishing with Bart and Justin. This might not be the worst start to summer after all!"

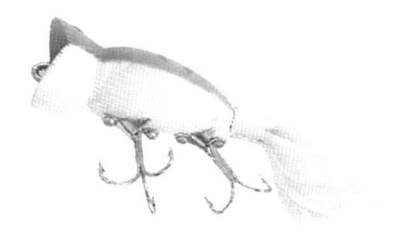

Chapter 2

We fly through breakfast. The whole time, my brain is scrambling. I try to think where all my fishing gear is in the garage. We give Mom a hug goodbye, then head out the laundry room door and into the garage.

"Be careful and have fun, you two!" Mom says as the door shuts behind us.

My awesome red bike is lying on its side and ready to go. Dad constantly tells me to stand it up, but I'm always in a hurry when

I get home. It doesn't seem to mind being on its side.

Crystal and I scurry around the garage and find our fishing rods and our green tackle box. We share a tackle box loaded with a bunch of great fishing lures. It's a good thing we didn't leave it at the cabin last summer. Now we can see how well the lures will do around here!

Crystal has her bike ready too. As she opens the garage door, I steady my bike. With my right hand, I grab my bike grip as well as my black fishing rod with the supercool blue-and-red spinning reel. With my left hand, I manage to dangle the tackle box and hold on to the handlebar. I point the rod forward so it clears the garage door. The last thing I want is to break my sweet rod. I love this thing.

Suddenly the door to the house opens, and Mom comes scooting out. "Hold your horses! Luke, you forgot your lucky hat," she says.

Mom walks up and slides my forest-green Cabela's hat on my head.

"Not only will this keep the sun out of your eyes, but it will also bring you luck," Mom says and smiles. "Not that you need any more luck, Mr. Lucky Luke. Crystal, do you want a hat?"

"Not a chance. I don't need a hat for luck," she says and then glides down the driveway.

"Gotta go," I say. "Bye, Mom!" I head out and race after Crystal.

"Have fun!" Mom yells.

I hit the curb at the end of the driveway a little fast, and the tackle box bounces and clunks loudly. I quickly look at the latch to make sure it's still shut. I don't want our tackle all over the street. Once I see that it's good to go, I race to catch up with Crystal.

We ride side by side down the street. The sun is shining, and there are only a couple of white fluffy clouds in the sky. The Minnesota air is warm, and I barely feel a breeze at all. What a perfect June day for fishing.

We race down the block. Then we cut through a sidewalk and jump into another street. We know this path well. Crystal and I spend as much time at Justin and Bart's house as they do at ours. We all practically live together.

We climb up the big hill next to the golf course. I look over and see a golfer take a big swing. He hits a line drive—right into a pond.

"Better luck next time!" I shout.

We hear the man laughing.

Onward we go, pushing up the big hill. Once we get to the top, we're both breathing hard.

After all that work getting *up* the hill, now we get the fun of going *down* it.

I stop pedaling, take a big breath, and start coasting down the other side. We pick up speed. Crystal and I have our heads down in a racing position. This is the best part of our ride. We see how long we can go without pedaling.

As we coast along, I realize that this is an adventure! Of course, I'm still bummed about not going to the cabin. But I have to admit that this day is shaping up to be a blast.

At the bottom of the hill, we look both ways before entering the street.

"No cars! We're good!" Crystal calls out.

We turn left across the main road and fly down our cousins' street. Still not pedaling but slowing down fast, I can see Justin and Bart's tan house ahead.

Now Crystal starts pedaling and takes the lead.

"See ya when you finally get there!" she yells.

I bear down and pedal harder. The race is on!

Chapter 3

I give the race everything I have, but it's no use. Crystal beats me and cruises into their front yard. She skids to a stop at the front door, raising her arms and fishing rod in victory. I come in hot and skid next to her.

The door opens, and Justin and Bart come out. They're carrying their rods and matching tan tackle boxes. Those were last year's Christmas presents.

"Hey, guys. How's it going?" Crystal asks.

"Good!" Bart replies.

Bart is a year younger than me and a little smaller. He has short brown hair and a round face like his dad's. Today he's wearing a green ball cap with his baseball team's logo on it.

Justin and I are the same age and same height. He has long brown hair. It almost touches his shoulders. He's sporting cool black sunglasses and a black rock-band T-shirt.

"That is *not* a fishing shirt," Crystal says, crinkling her face.

"Nope. But it'll work," Justin says.

"So, where exactly are we fishing?" I ask.

Bart and Justin exchange a little glance and smile.

"It's a secret!" Justin says. "We'll tell ya when we get there!"

"Let's go!" Bart exclaims, pointing with the hand holding his tackle box.

Crystal and I look at each other. We're both a little confused.

"Well, we're always looking for an adventure," Crystal tells me. "Now we're on one. Let's see where it takes us." She turns and follows after Justin and Bart.

In single file, we head around the house. We go through their backyard, which has way more trees than our yard does. These guys live on the edge of a park full of huge trees.

We climb the small hill at the back of their yard and pop up on the railroad tracks at the top. We start walking along the tracks, just like Huckleberry Finn.

Crystal and I keep looking back as we walk. We're a little nervous. We want to make sure a train isn't coming.

Justin sees our concerned looks. "The train only comes by at three in the afternoon," he says. "You're not going to get run over!"

That seems to help—a little. But I still keep my head on a swivel.

It isn't long until we slide down the other side of the hill and enter the park. Finally, I can see a lake through the woods. The blue water glistens in the sun and shines like diamonds. Instantly, I get the feeling there are a million hungry fish in that lake.

Please let this be where we're fishing! I think.

"There it is!" Justin confirms. "That's Hyland Lake. Our neighbor John is in high school at Jefferson. He told us this lake is loaded with largemouth bass. He's been fishing it for a few years." Justin's excitement is flowing now, and he picks up his pace toward the lake.

As we get closer, I see a finger of the lake cutting in toward us. If I try hard, I bet I can cast all the way across the water.

We quickly walk up to the water's edge. But then suddenly Justin slams on the brakes.

"Don't move! Look at that," he says. He carefully points next to a log in the water.

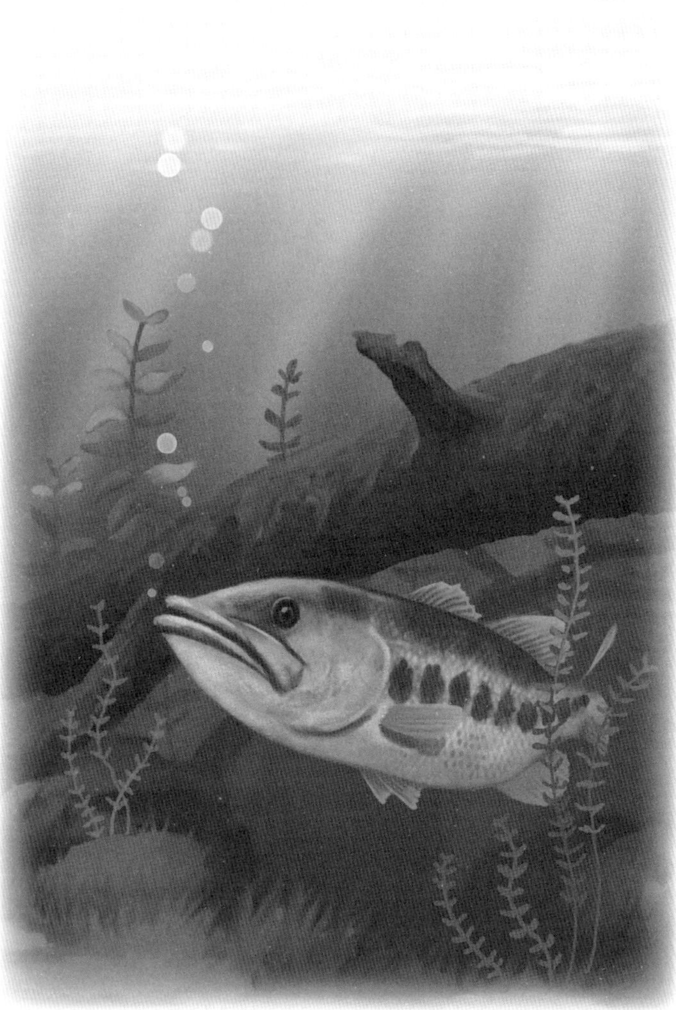

A giant bass is sitting there, underneath the log.

"Slowly back up," Justin whispers.

We all backpedal like elephants at the circus. We keep our focus on the fish. He doesn't move.

Once we're far enough back so the fish can't see us, we all race to get our fishing rods ready.

"Hold on," Crystal says. "We can't all go up there at once. We'll scare him away!" She looks at Justin. "You saw him first. You should get the first cast."

"Come on! That isn't fair!" Bart says.

"Well, what do you recommend instead?" Crystal asks Bart.

Bart thinks for a couple of moments but then shrugs. He can't come up with anything.

So, it's settled. Justin gets the first cast. He puts on a purple plastic worm for his lure, which we all agree should be perfect to get the bass to bite.

"You can do this, man!" I say, patting Justin on the back. "Go catch that monster."

"That's not a monster," says a strange voice from behind us. "That's Big Bubba!"

Chapter 4

We all whirl around at the same time, caught off guard. An older boy walks up to us. He has sandy-brown hair and is wearing black sunglasses and a faded jean jacket.

"Oh! Hey, John," Justin says and smiles. "These are my cousins, Luke and Crystal."

John nods to us. "Hi, guys. Nice to meet you."

Crystal and I give him a little wave and say hi.

John points out toward the water. "I've been trying to catch Big Bubba for two years," he says. "He's a legend around here. I had him once but lost him. He usually gives you one chance, and then he's gone. Well, Justin, let's see if you have what it takes to catch Big Bubba."

I can't see Justin's eyes under his sunglasses, but I'm guessing there's some nervousness in them. The bass is big and sounds impossible to catch, plus now we have a supercool older kid watching.

"Come on, man! You can do it," Crystal says as she gives Justin a thumbs-up.

As we all quietly cheer for Justin, he tiptoes up toward the water's edge.

John cups his mouth. "That's far enough," he whispers, just loud enough so Justin can hear.

Justin has his purple plastic worm in his left hand and his fishing rod in his right. He lets go of the lure, opens his bail to let the line loose, and holds his finger on the line. With a slow back-and-forth motion, he launches the worm out over the water, and it lands next to the log. Then he freezes, and we all stare at the ripple on the water.

Suddenly the line goes tight and pulls down toward the water's surface.

"Pull! You got him!" John yells, breaking the silence.

Justin closes the bail and cranks the handle. As the line gets tighter, he pulls back with all his might. The end of his rod bends down toward the water.

The fish on the other end takes off, and line starts screaming out of Justin's reel.

"Fish on!" Justin yells.

Then Bubba jumps out of the water and whips his head. The purple plastic worm shoots out of the fish's mouth and flies back toward us. We all duck so we don't get stuck by the hook.

Justin stands there and stares back at us. Apparently, he's in shock. He isn't saying a word.

I jump up and run over to him. "You *had* him, man!" I scan the lake for any sign of the fish. Nothing.

Justin's plastic worm crawls across the grass as he pulls in the line.

"That was epic!" John says with a giant smile and wild eyes. "You almost had Big Bubba."

"I don't know how I lost him," Justin says.

"Because he's giant and smart," John replies. "He spit that lure out like it was nothing. And now he's out of here—or at least for a while. Maybe he'll be back later."

When John sees our faces fall, he gives us a reassuring pep talk.

"But hey—there are still a bunch of other bass to catch out there. So get up to the bank and start casting!" He waves us on.

Without hesitating, I hurry up to the edge of the lake and launch a cast. Big Bubba may be gone, but that doesn't mean the fun is over.

I quickly reel in my silver Rapala. I get nothing on the first cast, so I try again.

Following my lead, everyone finds a spot around the shore and starts fishing. Bart is to my right, and Crystal and Justin are over on the left.

Bart launches his lure out to the middle of the small bay and starts to crank in his line. Instantly, something nails his lure, and he jerks back.

"Got one!" he yells.

After a short fight, he pulls in a small bass. It's about as long as my shoe. He holds it up proudly and then tosses it back into the water.

"Good job, Bart," I say. "Way to get the first fish!" I'm excited for him and eager to catch my first fish of the day.

I cast out again, then slowly start cranking in my lure. I give it a little twitch for more action.

Just then, a small bass comes racing up and takes a swipe at the lure. I pull, but nothing is there.

"Missed him!" I grunt.

I keep reeling. Another bass shoots up and nails my Rapala. Maybe it's the same fish I just missed. I quickly pull the rod to set the hook.

"Got him!" I howl.

The little dude jumps clear out of the water twice as I crank him in.

"Good job, Luke!" Justin yells over.

After I reel in the fish, I stick my right thumb in his mouth and squeeze with my pointer finger. I proudly pick him up, pop the hook out, and toss him back in.

After a few casts, Bart slides farther down the shore. He tosses his lure next to a weed clump, and a bass races out and clamps on. Bart yells and starts fighting with his second fish of the day.

"Yeah!" I hear Justin shout.

I look over, and Crystal is pulling in what seems to be a nice one. Bart and I watch as her rod goes crazy. With a snarl on her face, she fights the fish for a while and eventually pulls it up the bank and onto the grass. She squeals as the fish flops around like crazy.

She finally gets both hands over it and pulls her hook out. Then she holds it up for us to see. It's a super nice two-pound bass.

"That's a good one, Crystal!" I yell. "Way to go!"

We're all catching bass. It's totally epic.

I launch my Rapala out over the water again and slowly reel and jerk it. Two bass attack at the same time. I jerk back to set the hook just like the pros do on TV.

"Bam!" I say as I feel the tug. This fish is a fighter.

I finally slide him up to the edge of the lake and get a hold of him. This good-looking bass is close to two pounds. I hold him up and show Bart before tossing him back in.

I cast out again and pull in three bass back-to-back. I'm on fire!

When I look farther down the shoreline, I see John. He's standing alone and getting ready to cast. I can't wait to see what he catches!

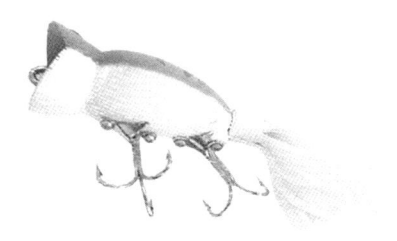

Chapter 5

John's lure lands with a splash. The water is perfectly calm since there isn't any wind.

John quickly pulls and cranks, then pulls and cranks again. The lure looks like it's swimming on top of the water.

Then, out of nowhere, a bass explodes from the water and bites the lure. John pulls hard and hooks the fish. The fight is on. John reels in the fish like a pro.

I walk over and watch him unhook the fish. It's huge. John smiles, gives the bass a nod of approval, and then tosses it back in.

"That was awesome!" I say to John. "That had to be three pounds."

"It was a good one, wasn't it?" he replies with a proud smile.

"Yeah. What did you catch him with?" I ask.

"This is a Hula Popper. It's supposed to be just like a frog. Bass love these things."

John shows me the lure. I've never seen anything like it before. It has a body, a skirt that looks like a frilly tail, and a flat front.

"The flat front makes the water swoosh when you pull it fast," John says. "That sound and the waves drive the bass crazy. This one is green and has black spots, just like a frog. You see that?" He holds it up closer to me.

"I do," I say. "That's cool!"

Then John casts it out again. I watch him jerk in the lure, and another bass crashes through the water and nails it. Without saying anything, John fights the bass and pulls it in. It's yet another three-pounder. He smiles, proudly shows me the fish, then tosses it back into the water.

In a matter of seconds, John has reeled in two bass that put all our little dudes to shame. Is it really all because of his Hula Popper?

I slide down past John and cast out my Rapala. Each time I reel in, the lure hooks weeds and gets tangled. I have to keep pulling off the weeds before I can cast again. I didn't have this kind of trouble earlier. But now I can't seem to get a decent cast at all.

"There are so many weeds just below the surface," John says. "You might be better off with a lure that doesn't go down so deep. That's why I love this Hula Popper."

"You're probably right," I say. "I should try something else."

My tackle box is over by Bart, so I head back.

"How's it going for you?" I ask Bart. I start digging in my tackle box for a new lure.

"I've caught seven so far," he says.

"Sweet!"

"Nothing big, though," he adds.

"Yeah, I hear ya on that," I reply, thinking about the monsters John pulled in.

I continue searching for a lure that floats. The only thing I see is my black plastic worm. Without a weight, it just might do the trick.

I bite my line and tie on a big hook. Then I slide the hook through the front of the worm. I pop out the hook about one inch down the body.

I turn toward the water and cast the worm out across the bay. The lure softly hits the surface, and little waves grow across the water until they disappear. Slowly I twitch the worm with a snap of my wrist.

After a few twitches, a small bass nails the worm. I set the hook hard and pull in the little guy.

So, at least the worm didn't sink into the weeds. And it's fun to catch another fish . . . but it's not as big as the bass John keeps catching with that Hula Popper.

"That settles it!" I declare loudly.

"That settles what?" Bart asks. He looks lost.

"Yeah," Crystal says as she and Justin walk over to us. "What are you talking about?"

"It's been awesome fishing here," I explain. "We're catching a ton of fish. But they're all small." I point down the shoreline toward John. "Meanwhile, John is over there, catching way bigger fish. We need Hula Poppers!"

"What the heck are Hula Poppers?" Crystal asks.

"They float on the surface and look like frogs," I say. "We need to get some. Now."

I pause dramatically and stare out into the water.

"And then we're gonna catch Big Bubba!"

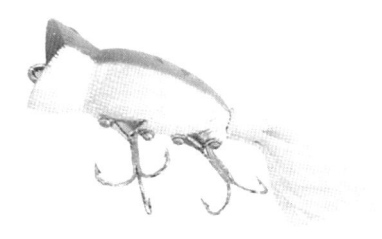

Chapter 6

We head back to Justin and Bart's house for lunch. While Aunt Patty makes us peanut butter and jelly sandwiches, we start planning how to get our hands on some Hula Poppers.

"I bet Burger Brothers has Hula Poppers," I say.

Crystal, Bart, and Justin nod in agreement.

Burger Brothers is our local sporting goods store. As far as I'm concerned, it's the greatest sporting goods store in the world.

"Hey, Mom," Justin says, "can you drive us over to Burger Brothers?"

"Burger Brothers?" she says, sliding the plate of sandwiches onto the table. "What in the world for?"

We all start talking at once. We tell her about fishing at the lake, Big Bubba, and John's Hula Popper.

"So, we *have* to get these lures, now!" Bart concludes.

Aunt Patty laughs but then shakes her head. "I'm sorry—I have a bunch of stuff to do around the house today. But why don't you kids just bike there?"

"Bike there?" Bart repeats. "But isn't it way down Ninety-Eighth Street? Like, miles away?"

"You guys ride your bikes everywhere, all day long," Aunt Patty says. "There's no reason you can't make it that far. You just make sure to bring your water bottles and your cell phones, and you'll be fine."

We're all quiet for a bit. We've gone to Burger Brothers a million times, just never on our bikes. But Aunt Patty is right. We ride everywhere, all the time.

I look across the table at Bart and Justin. "What do you guys think? Are you up for the challenge?"

"I'm game if you are," Justin says, chomping on his sandwich.

"Crystal?" I ask, turning to her next.

She shrugs. "Sure. Why not?"

"Sweet!" I say. "Then we're set for another adventure!"

Suddenly, I can't help but think of how much has changed since this morning. Only a few hours ago, I thought our summer fun was ruined because the trip to the cabin had been canceled. Yet here we are now, about to start another leg of our neighborhood adventure. This day is awesome!

Aunt Patty clears her throat, breaking my thoughts. "And do any of you have money to buy these Hula Popper thingies once you get there . . .?"

Crystal and I look at each other. "Did you bring any money?" I ask.

"Nope. I didn't think of that." She elbows Justin. "What about you guys?"

He just shakes his head.

Aunt Patty sighs and smiles. She grabs her red purse, sitting on the counter.

"Here's twenty dollars. Hopefully that should be enough!" she says, raising her shoulders and shaking her head.

"Awesome!" I exclaim. "Thank you, Aunt Patty. That's really nice of you."

I reach for the twenty, but Justin swoops in. He plucks it up and stuffs it in his pocket.

"I'll be in charge of that!" he says.

"Let's get rolling," Crystal announces. She stands up from the table. "We have a big ride ahead of us."

"Burger Brothers, here we come!" I say.

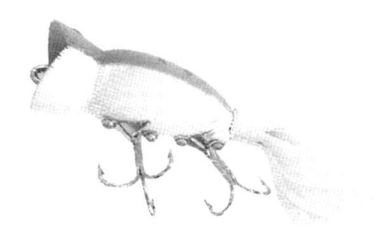

Chapter 7

We race down the street in a line of bikes. Justin leads the way. I'm behind him. Crystal is behind me. Bart is in the back.

We are *flying*. I have to pedal hard to keep up with Justin. After a few minutes I look back, and Crystal and Bart are falling behind.

"We better slow down so those guys can keep up," I call ahead to Justin.

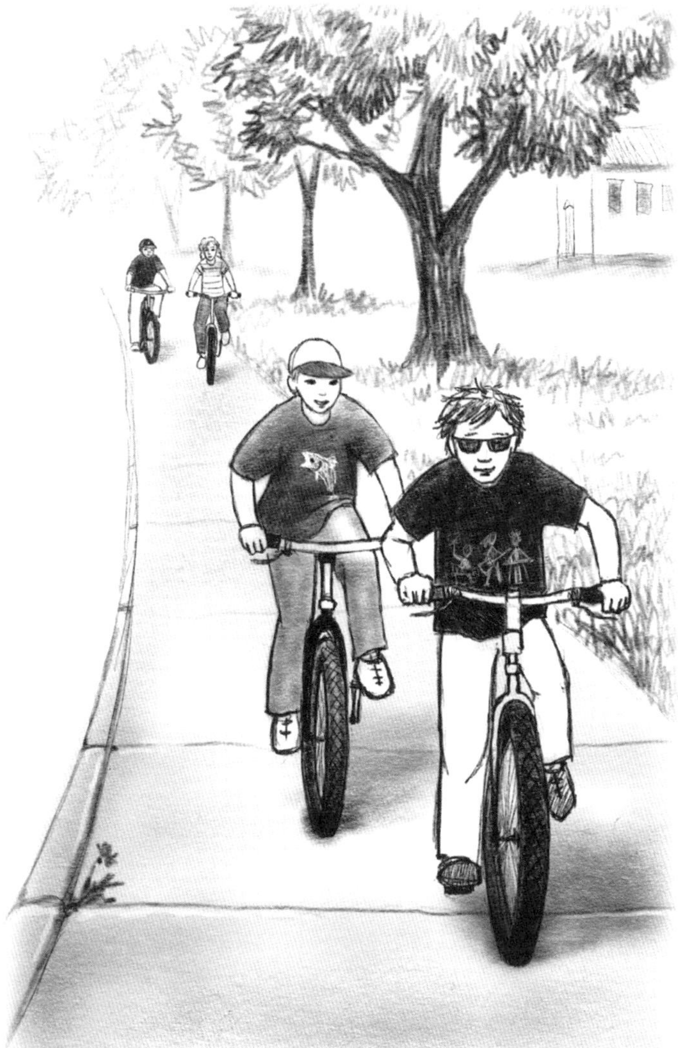

He looks back over his left shoulder.

"Oh, man. Come on, you guys!" he yells at the other two. He does slow a bit, though.

We zoom along the sidewalk and jump each curb as we cross street after street. Then it starts to sink in just how far away Burger Brothers really is. We've been pedaling for at least thirty minutes, yet we don't seem to be even halfway there.

"Wait up! We need a break!" Bart yells from behind.

Justin pulls over next to a big tree. Breathing hard, I skid to a stop next to him. I'm more than happy to take a break. Bart and Crystal pull up soon after.

"Wow," Bart says, wiping his brow. "This is a long way!"

"Yeah," I say, still catching my breath. "It's a little farther than I thought too. It never seemed this far in a car."

"We can do this, you guys," Crystal says. "Let's remember what this is all about. Luke seems to think these wonder Poppers will help us catch Big Bubba. Let's focus on that. Besides, the store can't be *that* much farther."

She looks down the street, and then we all turn to look with her. The only thing we can see are the golden arches of a McDonald's. Burger Brothers' famous green sign and brown building are nowhere in sight.

"Come on," Justin says. "Let's get on the road again." He pushes off and starts pedaling.

Immediately, that old Willie Nelson country song gets stuck in my head.

"On the road again," I sing. *"Just can't wait to get on the road again!"*

I belt the song as loud as I can. Then everyone joins in. None of us really know the other lyrics. We just repeat the same two lines, over and over.

We're still singing and pedaling like crazy when Justin suddenly lets out a whoop.

"There it is!" he calls out.

The familiar green sign of Burger Brothers appears in the distance.

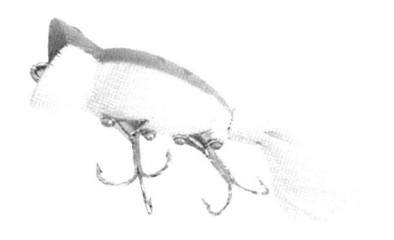

Chapter 8

We jump off our bikes and race inside. I scan the store for the fishing section and spot a bunch of black fishing rods lined up along a wall. I beeline my way to them.

"Hey, guys!" I call out. "I think the lures are back there." I point to the corner of the store.

We zigzag past camo jackets, bows and arrows, and tents. When we arrive in the fishing section, I stop to take stock of all the gear. There are rows and rows of tackle. There are different kinds of tackle for different kinds of fishing.

"Now all we need to do is find the row with bass tackle," I declare.

"Here's a bunch of spinnerbaits," Crystal says, walking past me.

It's a good sign. Spinnerbaits are used for bass fishing too.

In single file, we walk down the row. Sure enough, it's loaded with bass lures. There are plastic worms, spinnerbaits, jigs, and all kinds of other things. With our eyes wide open, we scan every lure.

"Look at all this cool stuff," Bart says.

Then a guy comes around the corner. I can tell he works here. He's wearing a cool green vest and a green fishing hat with a big hook stuck in it. His vest says *Larry*, and his big gray beard fits his clothing perfectly. He must be a great outdoorsman to be working here.

Suddenly, I'm imagining that we're not in our local sporting goods store. Instead, we're in a backwoods outfitter shop in some remote area out west. It adds to the sense of adventure.

"What can I help you find?" Larry asks with a friendly smile.

"Hula Poppers!" we all say at the same time.

Larry looks at us with bright eyes. His smile widens.

We all laugh.

"You kids sure know what you want!" he says. "Right this way." He motions for us to follow.

We turn into the next row and walk with purpose down to the other end. Without saying a word, Larry points to the display.

I look up, and my eyes burst wide open. There isn't just one Hula Popper to buy. There is a whole *section* of Hula Poppers. There are all kinds of sizes and colors displayed on the wall.

"Whoa . . ." Bart says slowly.

Larry steps aside, and we fight for position to see all the varieties of Hula Poppers.

"Which one would you recommend for catching the biggest bass in a lake?" I ask.

"The biggest bass, you say?" Larry repeats. "Well, let's take a look."

Stepping closer, he searches the display. His eyes start at the top and work their way down. Then he takes another run all the way through.

"This is what I would use to catch the biggest bass in the lake," Larry says. He grabs a green Hula Popper with black dots and a white tail.

"That's the kind John was using!" I say excitedly.

"It's a good one," Larry says. "They cost seven dollars and ninety-nine cents. How many do you guys want?"

Justin frowns, thinking hard. Then his eyes brighten, and he looks at each of us.

"How about we buy one to see how it works," he says. "Plus, that will leave us with enough money to stop at the McDonald's we passed. Ice cream sounds pretty good after that long ride. What do you guys think?"

"Oh, man. Ice cream versus Hula Poppers—that's a tough call," Bart says. He thinks for a moment. "I'm in for the ice cream."

Crystal and I nod in agreement. Now I have vanilla ice cream on my mind.

Justin takes the lure from Larry. We thank him and head to the counter to pay.

Back outside, we race to our bikes. Now that we have our Hula Popper, the journey continues. Ice cream, here we come!

After we finish our creamy vanilla ice cream, we get on our bikes and head back to Justin and Bart's house. It takes an hour of hard pedaling. During the entire ride, all I can think about is catching Big Bubba with that Hula Popper.

Can it happen?

Chapter 9

We finally pull into Justin and Bart's driveway. We're totally exhausted, yet we're still determined to get back to the lake and test out the Hula Popper before dark.

"All right, let's go get Big Bubba!" I say, trying to rally the troops.

"Wait," Crystal says. She eyes us one by one. "There are four of us and only one Hula Popper . . ."

I shrug. "So we take turns," I say.

"Yeah, but who gets the first turn?" Crystal asks.

No one says anything for a few moments. Then Justin lights up.

"I've got it!" he says. "Paper, rock, scissors."

We all agree that it seems fair. We circle up and start punching our fists on our open hands. "Paper, rock, scissors," we all chant together.

After three tries, it comes down to Justin and me.

"Paper, rock, scissors!" we chant. I go with paper, and he goes with rock.

"Yes! I get the first try!" I yell in victory.

Bart and Crystal just shake their heads.

"You are so lucky, Luke. There's no question about that," Bart says.

I'm totally relieved and fired up that I get to try first. If it works as well as I think it will, it may take only one cast to reel in Big Bubba.

I grab the Hula Popper and race to tie it on my line. I chomp through my line with ease. Then I quickly use my mouth and fingers to spin a perfect fisherman's knot.

"Ready!" I yell. I raise my right hand just like a rodeo cowboy would.

With our new Hula Popper tied on my line, we march toward the railroad tracks.

We are ready for more action. I can't wait to make that first cast.

The sun is low in the sky as we approach the magical lake. Squinting from the sunlight, I see the sunken log Big Bubba was under this morning. We slow down.

"All right, Luke. Make this count," Justin coaches me.

I crouch down so the fish won't see me. I creep forward and get into position. When I'm about ten steps from the lake, I get down on my knees.

I look back at the gang. Justin gives me a thumbs-up. Crystal and Bart nod in agreement.

I carefully unhook the Hula Popper from an eyelet on my rod. Then I pick out a spot on the lake and aim my cast. I arch back my rod and launch the Hula Popper.

But the lure shoots up, flying way higher than I had planned. Then, instantly, it stops.

I look up, and my heart sinks.

Our one and only Hula Popper is stuck in a branch hanging down about ten feet in front of me.

Chapter 10

"Noooo!" Justin and Bart groan at the same time. Not too loud, though, so they don't scare the fish.

My eyes lock on the lure in total disbelief. I quickly tug and jerk the line to see if I can pull it loose. It doesn't budge. It's stuck for good.

My head sinks, and my shoulders drop. I feel complete defeat, like when I get rained out of a baseball game.

Bart slides in next to me. "Well, that technically counts as the first cast," he says with a not-so-sorry smile. "So, I guess it's someone else's turn now!"

I stare at him, still in utter disbelief. "I guess you're right," I say. "But at least let me get the Hula Popper down so we can use it. I believe it's our best bet to catch Big Bubba, if he's out there."

All our eyes follow my fishing line up and stare at the brand-new Hula Popper stuck high on the big branch.

"Oh boy. What's your plan, Luke?" Justin asks.

My eyes go from the branch, over to the tree, and down the trunk. "It looks like I have to climb the tree."

"No way, Luke," Crystal says, shaking her head. "That is way too high to climb."

"I have to," I say. "There's no way I'm gonna leave our lure up there."

"Well, I guess we've done crazier things than climb a tree like that," Bart says.

"That's for sure," Justin agrees.

We walk over to the base of the tree, and I start planning my climb.

"All I have to do is get to that branch," I say, pointing. "And then the rest will be a breeze."

I reach up and stand on my tiptoes. The branch is only a couple of feet above my outstretched fingertips.

"Justin, I need you, buddy," I say, looking back at him.

"Here we go again," he says. He shakes his head and laughs. "It's always something, isn't it, Luke?"

Without hesitating, Justin gets down on all fours next to the tree. Bart and Crystal move in to help.

"Oh, you guys are crazy!" Crystal says.

"That's what makes it so much fun," Bart says, smiling. "Come on, Luke. Get up there."

I carefully step on Justin's back with my right foot and then my left. Crystal and Bart both push me up to take some of the weight off Justin. He grunts, and we all pause.

"I'm good!" Justin says.

I stretch as far as I can and reach for the branch. I can just barely touch it.

"Push! Come on, push!" I plead to Bart and Crystal.

Bart growls. He and Crystal give me a giant shove. My chest jams against the tree, and the rough bark scrapes me as I inch higher. With all my might, I grab the branch and lift myself off Justin's back.

Then Justin jumps up, turns toward the tree, and gets my feet onto his shoulders. When he shoves me up, I almost launch into the tree.

"Whoa!" I say. "Sweet! Good job down there."

I look down and see Justin and Bart high-five.

"Teamwork!" Bart says.

I refocus on my task and see the Hula Popper at the end of a branch. It's time to get that baby down.

I've climbed a hundred trees, so this is no problem. I quickly make my way up. I grab each branch and make sure my feet are secure before moving to the next.

I stop when I make it to the branch with my lure on it. This next part will be a little scary. I need to walk on the branch, but it's pretty thin and long, and my lure is way out there. I'm not sure the branch is strong enough for my weight.

"Don't do it, Luke!" Crystal calls up.

"I *have* to get Hula Popper," I call down. I keep my eyes on the branch and lure.

"Careful, man," Justin says.

I test the branch by standing on it while also holding on to a limb above my head. This way, I can control how much weight I put on it. Then I carefully rock up and down. The branch seems strong. It better be, for my sake.

I slide my feet out along the branch, away from the main trunk. The branch bends slightly, but I'm still feeling good about this. Like a snake, I straddle the branch and inch my way out.

I can hear Crystal squealing with fear for me. I don't look down; I just focus on the lure.

After several scoots, I reach out and touch the stranded Hula Popper. I carefully unhook it from the bark and let it fall to the ground.

"Yeah!" Bart howls. "Good job, Luke! You did it!"

Crystal and Justin cheer for me too.

Even though I'm pumped that we have the lure back, I keep focused on the branch. I carefully ease myself back to the main trunk. Finally, I grab hold of a bigger branch that I know will support me.

"Now, *that* was awesome!" I yell down. I give the gang a thumbs-up.

"Get down here, you crazy nut!" Crystal says.

Before I start climbing down, I take a moment to look down at the lake. I realize I can see right through the clear water. Scanning the shoreline, I spy a bunch of fallen branches, rocks, and clumps of weeds.

"This is amazing! I can see right into the water from up here," I report.

Then my eyes pop open. I can see a huge bass swimming toward our shoreline. It's just like my dream from this morning.

"Guys, there's a giant bass swimming our way!" I yell. "I think it might be Big Bubba!"

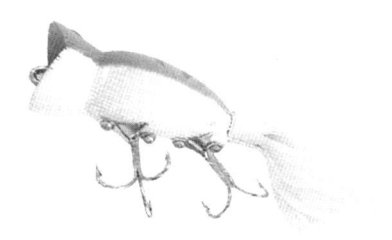

Chapter 11

Everyone freezes for a moment.

"No way. Really?" Justin says, looking up at me.

"Yes, really!" I yell back. "Get your rods ready."

Justin and Bart race for their rods.

"Crystal, use my fishing rod," I say. "That Hula Popper might be the ticket."

Without hesitating, Crystal steps over, picks up my rod, and reels in the line.

"Where is he?" Bart says, scanning the water like a hawk.

"Straight out," I reply.

I keep scanning the water too. From up here, I feel like a sailor on a whaling ship.

"I think Crystal should cast the Hula Popper just past the big tree branch," I say.

I can hear Bart and Justin coaching Crystal. She's getting ready to make the perfect cast.

"Now, Crystal! He's just sitting out there," I call down.

"Here goes nothing!" she says.

She pulls the rod back and launches it forward. The Hula Popper flies through the air.

I see it all in slow motion. The moment the lure hits the water, Big Bubba circles and shoots right at it. But then he stops two feet from it. I can tell he's staring at it.

"Crystal, he's looking right at it," I coach from my perch. "Give the rod a twitch. Make him think the lure is alive."

The second she moves the Hula Popper, Big Bubba attacks. He opens his huge mouth and swallows it.

"Pull!" I scream. "Pull!"

Crystal jerks back and sets the hook. Big Bubba shoots out of the water, leaping way up into the air. I gasp and watch his massive head shake back and forth. He's trying to spit the hook out, like before. But when he lands, Crystal's line still stretches out into the water.

"You still have him!" I bark. "Fight him!"

Justin and Bart both cheer Crystal on. I can't stop hooting and hollering from my bird's-eye view. This is epic.

Big Bubba keeps taking out line. I can hear the drag on my reel screaming. Crystal pulls and fights, just like Dad taught us to do.

With one giant jump after another, Big Bubba does everything he can to get loose.

I catch movement to my right. A couple of kids are running through the woods toward us. Clearly, they hear the excitement.

Two boys run up and join the cheering. They look older than us, and then I realize one is John. This is so cool!

Finally, Crystal pulls Big Bubba right up to the edge of the water. It looks like he's done fighting.

John runs right into the lake with his shoes on. He stops when the water reaches his knees.

"Pull him right to me. I'll grab him for you," John says, still a little out of breath.

Crystal eases the fish to her right, and Big Bubba glides straight into John's waiting hand. He sticks his thumb into the giant fish's mouth and pulls him up out of the water.

Everyone erupts in cheers, especially me. I'm sure the whole neighborhood can hear us.

I can't wait to see the giant bass, so I slither down the tree like a jaguar. Launching from a branch that's probably a bit too high, I hit the ground and roll to break my fall. I run over to Crystal and give her a huge high five.

She has a giant smile stuck to her face.

Everyone circles around John and touches the massive fish.

"He must be seven pounds," John says. "Does anyone have a cell phone?"

"Yep," says Crystal.

"Let's quickly take a picture of this guy," John says. "Then we can get him back in the water. We want to treat him right. He's an old fish."

Crystal pulls out her phone and hands it to Justin. "Will you take the picture?" she asks.

"Absolutely!" says Justin.

"Okay, slide your thumb into his mouth," John instructs as he hands the fish off to Crystal. "His teeth are like sandpaper, but they won't hurt you."

"I've held small bass before," she says. "But never anything this big." She looks a little nervous.

"You can do it," John encourages.

Crystal reaches over and grabs the giant by his bottom lip. Then John dries his hand on his jeans and takes the phone from Justin.

"Everyone get over there," John directs us. "You all have to be in the picture."

With big smiles, we huddle around Crystal as John snaps several photos.

"Okay!" John says. "Now let's get him back into the water."

We follow Crystal to the shore, and she carefully slides Big Bubba into the shallow water. She puts her hands on each side of the fish to keep him upright. With one giant flip of his tail, he splashes Crystal in the face and rockets into the middle of the lake. Crystal squeals, flinches, and looks at us with a face drenched in water.

"Well, that was rude of him!" she says.

We all burst out laughing.

As we head back to Justin and Bart's house, I'm in my own little world. I think about all the crazy adventures we had today. And it was all right here, not far from home.

The best part is that we still have the whole summer ahead of us. I wonder what other awesome adventures we will come up with!

About the Author

Kevin Lovegreen was born and raised in Minnesota. His loving wife, Sue and two amazing children, Crystal and Luke all share their love for the outdoors. Hunting and fishing have always been a big part of Kevin's life. From chasing squirrels as a child to chasing elk as an adult, Kevin loves the thrill of the adventure. But even more, he loves telling the stories. Presenting at schools and connecting with kids is one of his favorite things to do.

Lucky Luke's 25 lb. turkey

Monster Mule Deer

The Muddy Elk

Crystal's 1st buck

Lucky Luke with a large-mouth bass

Lucky Luke's 1st bear

Crystal, The Swamp hero!

www.KevinLovegreen.com

Other books in the series

AR-rated
(Accelerated Reader)

Award-winning

To order books or learn about school visits please go to: **www.KevinLovegreen.com**

LUCKY LUKE'S ADVENTURES

Dear reader,

I hope you enjoyed the adventure!

All the stories in the Lucky Luke's Adventure series are based on real experiences. And I truly believe they all happened so I could write you these books.

If you like this book, please help spread the word by telling all your friends.

      Keep being amazing!

Kevin Lovegreen

**The More You Read,
The Smarter You Get!**